The War of the Worlds

H.G. Wells

SADDLEBACK
PUBLISHING

Saddleback's *Illustrated Classics*™

SADDLEBACK
PUBLISHING
www.sdlback.com

ISBN-13: 978-1-56254-952-7
ISBN-10: 1-56254-952-9
eBook: 978-1-60291-175-8

Printed in Guangzhou, China
1012/CA21201293

16 15 14 13 12   2 3 4 5 6

Welcome to
Saddleback's *Illustrated Classics*™

We are proud to welcome you to Saddleback's *Illustrated Classics*™. Saddleback's *Illustrated Classics*™ was designed specifically for the classroom to introduce readers to many of the great classics in literature. Each text, written and adapted by teachers and researchers, has been edited using the Dale-Chall vocabulary system. In addition, much time and effort has been spent to ensure that these high-interest stories retain all of the excitement, intrigue, and adventure of the original books.

With these graphically *Illustrated Classics*™, you learn what happens in the story in a number of different ways. One way is by reading the words a character says. Another way is by looking at the drawings of the character. The artist can tell you what kind of person a character is and what he or she is thinking or feeling.

This series will help you to develop confidence and a sense of accomplishment as you finish each novel. The stories in Saddleback's *Illustrated Classics*™ are fun to read. And remember, fun motivates!

Overview

Everyone deserves to read the best literature our language has to offer. Saddleback's *Illustrated Classics*™ was designed to acquaint readers with the most famous stories from the world's greatest authors, while teaching essential skills. You will learn how to:

- Establish a purpose for reading
- Activate prior knowledge
- Evaluate your reading
- Listen to the language as it is written
- Extend literary and language appreciation through discussion and writing activities.

Reading is one of the most important skills you will ever learn. It provides the key to all kinds of information. By reading the *Illustrated Classics*™, you will develop confidence and the self-satisfaction that comes from accomplishment—a solid foundation for any reader.

Step-By-Step

The following is a simple guide to using and enjoying each of your *Illustrated Classics™*. To maximize your use of the learning activities provided, we suggest that you follow these steps:

1. ***Listen!*** We suggest that you listen to the read-along. (At this time, please ignore the beeps.) You will enjoy this wonderfully dramatized presentation.

2. ***Post-reading Activities.*** You have successfully read the story and listened to the audio presentation. Now answer the multiple-choice questions and other activities in the Study Guide.

Remember,

"Today's readers are tomorrow's leaders."

H.G. Wells

Herbert George Wells, an English novelist, historian, journalist, and author of science fiction stories, was born in 1866. His father was a shopkeeper, and his mother worked occasionally as a housekeeper. After completing his early formal schooling, Wells worked as a teacher. He later received a scholarship to study at a school with a special focus on the sciences.

His training as a scientist is shown in his imaginative science fiction stories. Wells described trips in airplanes and submarines when such modes of transportation had not yet been invented. *The Time Machine* describes a trip into the future, and *The War of the Worlds* is an account of an invasion from Mars. Several of his science fiction works have been the basis of popular movies.

Though he is best known for his science fiction stories, Wells wrote a variety of other works. He was a strong believer in education and wrote three lengthy books in which he tried to bring important ideas in history and science to the general public. His numerous books, articles, and essays also show his bold support of social change.

H.G. Wells died in 1946.

H. G. Wells

The War of
the Worlds

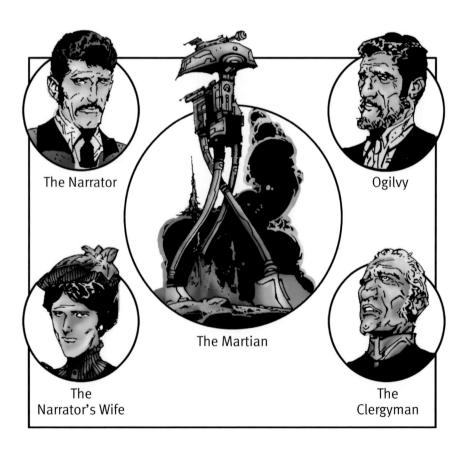

The Narrator

Ogilvy

The
Narrator's Wife

The Martian

The
Clergyman

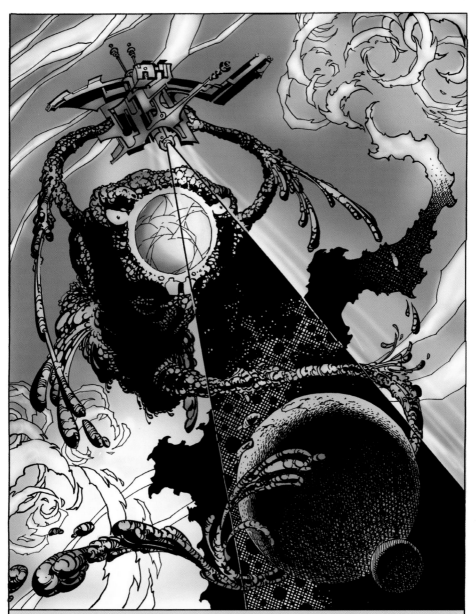

No one believed in the late 1800s that this world was being watched by creatures smarter than man. Yet far off in space, such creatures did watch this earth and made plans to attack us.

In the late 1800s, astronomers of the world were excited by a report of a large explosion upon the planet Mars. A great ball of fire was speeding toward the earth. Besides a few small notices in the newspapers, no one seemed to worry about the danger coming toward us.

I heard of it only by a chance meeting with Ogilvy, an astronomer friend.

It's most exciting! Come up tonight and take a look through my telescope.

Thanks, I'll be there.

That night I saw another explosion of gas, just at midnight.

There's a reddish flash—a sort of streamer coming toward us.

Quick—let me look!

Yes...I see it... remarkable!

Is it possible there are living creatures on Mars who are signaling toward us?

Nonsense! The chances of anything man-like on Mars are a million to one. It's probably a heavy shower of meteorites or a volcanic explosion.

And so, the Martian ships rushed earthward, nearer day by day.

Then came the night of the first falling star. Many people saw it, including Ogilvy.

A meteorite! And nearby!

Very early in the morning he started in search of it.

I am sure it lies this way...somewhere on the common.

Smoke! It has set the field on fire.

Amazing! A cylinder! Most meteorites are round.

At first the heat kept Ogilvy at a distance.

A clicking noise! I suppose it's the metal cooling...

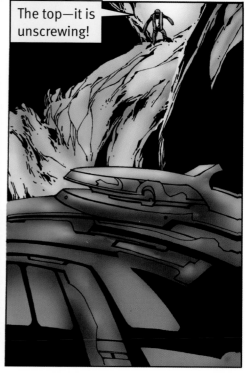

The top—it is unscrewing!

In a flash it came to him—the cylinder was hollow! There was something inside!

Good heavens! I bet there's a man in it—half roasted—trying to escape!

I must help him!

In a moment, he knew this thing had something to do with the flash on Mars.

No— too hot!

Climbing out of the pit, he ran toward the town of Woking to get help. The first person he saw was Henderson, a reporter for a London newspaper, who was tending his garden.

You saw that shooting star last night?

Yes?

It's out on Horsell Common now!

What? A fallen meteorite.

As the two men hurried back to the common, Ogilvy told Henderson what he had seen.

It's in the same place but the top is nearly out!

You can hear air entering or escaping!

They tapped on the metal with a stick but got no answer.

I say in there, hold tight! We'll go for more help.

Poor fellows, they're probably out cold.

Unable to do anything themselves, they returned to town for more help.

We must get workmen with shovels.

I must telegraph my paper!

The news spread swiftly. I heard it when I went to get my daily newspaper.

Men from Mars, they say...out on the common!

What? Impossible!

Startled, I hurried to see for myself. A small crowd had gathered to watch.

The top of the cylinder—it's being unscrewed from inside!

It's out!

Keep back, everyone! We don't know what's in there!

I think everyone expected to see a man come out—I know I did. But what I saw in the shadow were two glowing circles, like eyes. Then something like a gray snake coiled up and wriggled in the air toward me.

A woman screamed. I felt the crowd behind me moving back. I stood frozen as more of the tentacles came out.

A big grayish bulk was rising slowly and painfully out of the cylinders. Two large eyes looked at me steadily.

Suddenly the monster fell over the rim into the pit, with a thud and an odd cry; and another of the creatures appeared in the opening.

I ran madly for a group of trees, stumbling for I could not stop watching.

There among the trees I stood and watched, fearful but interested.

Thin black whips, like the arms of an octopus, flashed across the sunset.

Then a thin rod rose up, joint by joint, with a round plate spinning at the top.

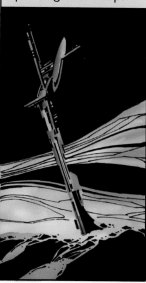

I saw a small group of men moving toward the pit. The leader was waving a white flag.

They decided to try to talk with the Martians. The flag waved to the right...to the left...

There was a flash of light. Green smoke rose from the pit in three puffs, straight into the air.

Slowly a shape rose out of the pit and a beam of light shot out from it...

A blinding jet of light! As it hit each man he fell and lay still; pine trees and the dry grass burst into flames.

I could not move. If that beam of light had gone a little bit further, I too would be dead.

But it missed me and passed, and left the night about me dark and unfriendly.

Suddenly I was afraid. I turned and began a stumbling run through the field.

Behind, nearly forty bodies lay under the starlight about the pit, among them Ogilvy and Henderson.

I remember nothing of my flight except my fear. Finally I staggered and fell by the side of the road.

As last I rose and walked shakily away, my everyday self again. The silent common and my flight were like a dream.

Over the Mayberry bridge a train went flying south. I heard voices from a nearby yard. It was all so familiar—but what of that flaming death behind me!

I stopped at a group of people.

What news from the common?

Haven't you been there?

What's it all about?

Haven't you heard of the men from Mars—the creatures from Mars?

Quite enough, thanks!

I felt foolish and angry. I tried and found I could not even tell them what I had seen.

You'll hear more yet!

At home, I told my wife what I had seen. The dinner lay on the table.

There is one thing—they may keep the pit and kill those who come near, but they cannot get out of it.

They may come here!

No, they can hardly move! Earth's gravity is three times that of Mars. So a Martian here weighs three times more than on Mars, but his strength doesn't change.

After I had wine and food, I felt much better.

They probably did this terrible thing because they were so afraid.

If worse comes to worst, a bomb dropped into the pit will kill them all.

I did not know it, but that was the last peaceful dinner I was to eat for many strange and terrible days.

I had forgotten the fact that the Martians had enough mechanical skill to overcome the heaviness of their bodies. All night long they worked on the machines they would use.

About eleven that night, two companies of soldiers arrived and formed a line along the edge of the common.

A few seconds after midnight a star fell—the second cylinder.

The next day was one of suspense. The milkman came as usual...

What news?

The Martians were surrounded by troops during the night. They're not to be killed, if possible.

And they say another one of those things has fallen—but one's enough, surely!

This whole thing will cost the insurance people plenty before everything's settled!

After breakfast I walked down toward the common. Near the bridge I met some soldiers.

Sorry, sir...no one allowed past here.

None of them had seen the Martians. I told them what I knew of the Heat-Ray.

Crawl up under cover and rush them, I say.

What's cover against their heat? Why not shell them straight off and finish them!

I returned home, having learned nothing new. It was a very warm day and we had supper outside.

Suddenly there was firing—and a violent, rattling crash that shook the ground.

We saw the tops of the nearby trees burst into flame, and the tower of the little church slide down into ruin.

The top of our hill must be within range of the Heat-Ray!

One of our chimneys cracked as if a shot had hit it, and a piece tumbled down.

We can't possibly stay here!

But where are we to go?

To your cousins' in the town of Leatherhead!

Down the hill I saw a group of soldiers galloping. Two got off their horses and began running from house to house.

Everybody out! You must leave! Get out!

Quickly I ran to the village inn, knowing the landlord had a horse and a cart.

I'll give you two pounds and bring it back by midnight!

All right! What's the hurry?

I rushed home, packed a few valuables into the cart, and jumped into the driver's seat beside my wife.

Soon we were clear of the smoke and noise. Ahead was a quiet, sunny land-scape. The hedges on either side were sweet with roses.

At the top of a hill I looked back at streamers of black smoke shot with red fire. Already smoke was far away to east and west. The Martians were setting fire to everything within range of their Heat-Ray.

We reached Leatherhead with no trouble and were welcomed by my wife's cousins.

Come in!

What's happened?

After an hour's rest for the horse, I left my wife in their care and started to return.

The night was dark and close; the clouds heavy. My wife stood in the light of the doorway. Her face was very white.

The houses I passed were black and silent. I heard midnight ring out from a church tower behind me.

Suddenly a green light filled the road. The clouds were pierced by a thread of green fire. The third cylinder had fallen in a field to my left.

Thunder and lightning burst like a rocket overhead. The horse ran away.

We trotted alone, lightning flashing around us, rain beating at my face. At first I watched only the road.

Suddenly I saw something moving rapidly down the hill on the other side.

This thing I saw! How can I describe it? A monstrous tripod, stepping over the pine trees and smashing them aside; a walking engine of shining metal.

Then the trees ahead of me were parted, and a second tripod appeared. I was galloping hard to meet it!

I pulled the horse's head hard to the right.

In another moment the cart had turned over. I was flung sideways into a pool of water.

I crawled out and hid under a bush. The thing went walking by me, and passed uphill.

As it passed it began to howl and in another moment joined its companion half a mile away.

Aloo! Aloo!

They bent over something in the field, no doubt the third cylinder. For some minutes I watched them move about in the distance.

Finally, crawling in a ditch, I made it into a pine woods.

My only wish was to reach my house and at last, tired, I did so.

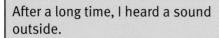

After a long time, I heard a sound outside.

Come in, if you want to hide.

Yes! Please!

You're a soldier! What's happened?

They wiped us out—simply wiped us out!

I'm a cannon driver. We were moving our guns up to the sand pit...

My horse stepped in a hole and came down. It threw me into a ditch.

The gun exploded behind me and the shells blew up; there was fire and death all around. I was buried under everything.

I lay still for a long time, scared out of my wits.

Finally I got away, and somehow I reached here.

Upstairs we looked out of the window across the valley. The early morning light showed the ruins—and three metallic giants looking down at the damage they had done.

We agreed the house was no place to stay.

I want to rejoin my troop.

I must find my wife and take her to safety!

We filled our pockets with food, then we sneaked out.

We cut through a woods and reached a road where we saw an officer on a horse.

Trying to rejoin my troop, sir. Martians are along the road here!

What are they like?

Giants made of metal, sir. A hundred feet high. With a box that shoots fire.

Nonsense!

But it's true!

The soldiers were trying to clear people out of their houses. They were having trouble.

You can't take those, sir!

My flowers! They're valuable!

Do you know what's over there?

Eh?

Death! Death is coming!

Across a flat meadow we saw six big guns with gunners standing by.

They will get one fair shot, at least.

It's bows and arrows against the lightning!

Every likely spot between here and London will hide a gun. We'll stop them!

The Martians came. We ran for cover.

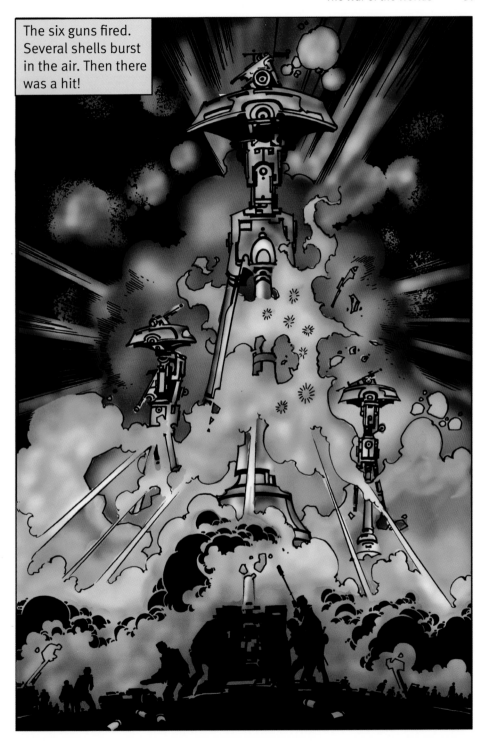

The Martian stumbled and went down.

His companion turned his Heat-Ray on the troops. Guns and ammunition flashed into fire.

The fallen Martian crawled from his hood and began repairs.

He mended the leg as easily as we might mend our clothes!

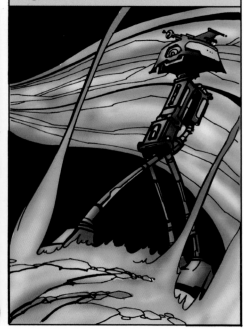

After the guns were blown up and the nearby woods and buildings set afire, people ran in every direction. At last I crawled under a hedge, tired, and fell asleep.

When I awoke there was a clergyman seated beside me.

Have you any water?

No! No!

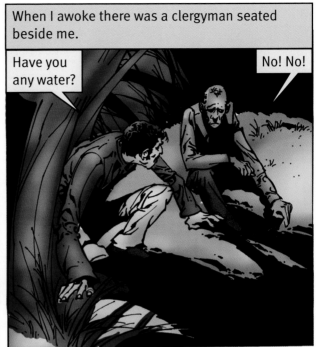

I was walking to clear my brain and suddenly—fire, earthquake, death!

It's the End—Judgment Day! Man is punished for his sins!

All these terrible happenings had almost driven him mad.

Suddenly we saw two Martians.

Knowing that many hidden guns were waiting for the Martians, I expected to hear firing—and to see the deadly Heat-Rays aimed.

Instead the Martians used another terrible weapon—the Black Smoke!

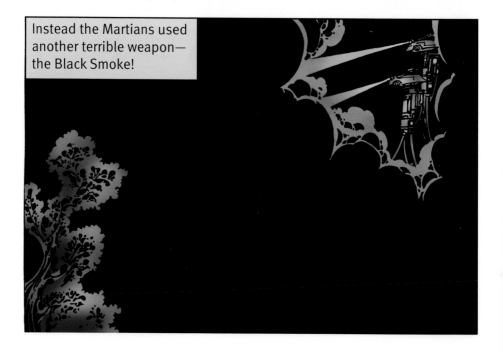

The deadly smoke poured over the ground, streamed into the valleys, flowed into every crack. To breathe it meant death.

When all were dead, the Martians cleared the air by spraying a jet of steam upon it.

So, as men might smoke out a wasp's nest, the Martians spread this deadly smoke over the country toward London. Wherever guns might be hidden, they used the Black Smoke.

Soon news of the Martians and terrible fear reached London. My younger brother was there, and he told me later of his experiences.

Danger! Suffocation! Black Smoke!

The Martians are able to shoot out clouds of a poisonous smoke...they have wiped out our troops...and are heading towards London. There is no safety but retreat.

Commander-in-Chief

Panic hit London. The six million people started running northward.

My brother reached the coast and found a space on an already crowded ship. Fishing boats and other boats were picking up passengers.

They had already left the coast when a Martian appeared, small in the distance.

It was the first Martian my brother had seen and he stood amazed, watching it come toward them.

The Captain called for full speed, but they seemed to move with terrifying slowness.

Suddenly the steamboat lurched, throwing my brother off his feet.

About a hundred yards away an iron ship tore through the water.

It was a torpedo-ram steaming headlong toward the Martian.

The guns of the torpedo-ram fired.

The Martian pointed his Heat-Ray at the torpedo-ram. With a violent flash, the ship was destroyed.

A great cloud of steam arose to hide everything from sight as the little ship continued out to sea.

It was getting dark when the Captain cried out and pointed.

Look!

It was the fourth cylinder rushing through the darkness.

48

After the Martians had used the Black Smoke, during the panic in London and my brother's adventures, the clergyman and I had hidden in an empty house.

Later...

The Black Smoke is gone! We can leave now.

No, no! It is safe here!

But I knew I must go.

I must find my wife!

Don't leave me alone!

Suddenly we saw a Martian.

He was following people but he was not using the Heat-Ray.

Instead he was picking them up...

and tossing them into a metal cage!

Seeing this, we ran as fast as we could into a ditch.

It was late at night before we dared come out.

I don't see anything.

We stayed off the road, sneaking along hedges and through bushes.

We went into an empty house searching for food. We were hungry and thirsty.

Here's bread and ham!

There's water...

Suddenly, as we ate, a blinding green light filled the sky, and an explosion such as I had never heard before sent everything flying.

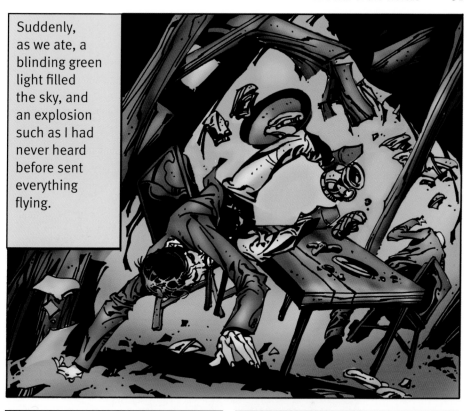

When I came to we were in darkness.

Shh! Don't move! They are outside!

Until morning came, we hardly moved. Then we saw, through a hole in the wall, the body of a Martian standing guard.

The fifth cylinder! The fifth shot from Mars has hit this house and buried us under ruins!

God have mercy on us!

At first I was afraid to breathe. Then hunger drove us to the kitchen to find food. Through a crack we watched the Martians as they built their awful machines. So the days passed...

On the ninth day, a sudden noise awoke me from a nap. I saw the body of the clergyman on the floor—and a long metallic arm feeling its way over the fallen beams!

I quickly slipped through the door of the coal-cellar into the darkness there. Had the Martian seen me?

There was movement...tapping...a dragging sound. I peeped into the kitchen. The Martian was taking the clergyman away.

I crawled into the coal and tried to cover myself.

I heard the Martian playing with the door knob!

The door opened. It felt its way toward me.

It touched my shoe. I bit my hand to keep from screaming.

It picked up a lump of coal to look at.

It then pulled back. The door closed. Then silence!

It came no more. But I lay for another day in the darkness before thirst made me find water.

Nothing— and no noise outside!

At last I dared to look through the peephole. The pit was empty!

I climbed out of the pit.

The day seemed very bright. The sky was blue. Not a Martian was in sight.

I started toward London through the countryside looking for food.

I saw a cat slip into a doorway, frightened by me.

Then it was a rat that fled.

I remembered hiding in a ditch!

And burying myself in the coal.

Just like the animals, I would have to run. To hide from every noise and every creature that passed my way. The Martians now controlled the earth.

For two days I wandered, finding little food, seeing no human being.

I reached London, I saw no one about. I wandered the streets feeling like the last man left on earth.

It was near South Kensington that I first heard the howling.

Uh-la
Uh-la
Uh-la.

It was a lonely inhuman sound.

I couldn't imagine what it could be.

Terror filled me and I ran.

Suddenly—a Martian!

Uh-la.
Uh-la.
Uh-la.

The sound stopped. Silence came like thunder. The hood fell forward.

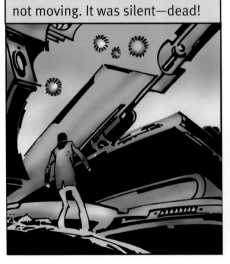

I ran toward the monster. It was not moving. It was silent—dead!

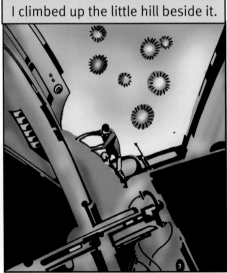

I climbed up the little hill beside it.

The Martians were dead! Here and there they were lying, nearly fifty altogether, overtaken by a death they could not understand.

They had been killed by the smallest things that God has put upon this earth—disease bacteria!

There are no bacteria on Mars. The Martians' bodies were unprepared. As soon as they arrived on earth, our tiny bacteria began their overthrow.

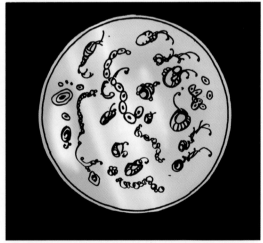

Disease had killed the Martians—just as it had killed many men before we had learned to overcome it.

Telegraph keys flashed the joyful news all over the world.

Church bells told the news, too, until all England was bell-ringing.

I boarded one of the free trains that were taking people home.

And so I came back at last.

My study window was open as I had left it.

Our muddy footprints still went up the stairs.

And on my desk was the work I had left behind.

I went downstairs. No one had been here. The faint hope I had was foolish.

Then a strange thing occurred.

It is no use. No one has been here.

Had I spoken my though aloud? I turned, and the French window was open behind me.

There, amazed and afraid even as I, were my cousin and my wife!

My wife put her hand to her throat and swayed. I made a step forward and caught her in my arms.

I came, I knew— I knew!

Strange it is to hold my wife's hand again, and to think that I had thought her, and that she had thought me, among the dead.

Our thoughts about the human future must be greatly changed by these happenings. We have learned that we cannot think of this planet as being fenced in. If the Martians can reach another planet, there is no reason to think that everyone can't travel in space. Wonderful is the idea I have seen in my mind, of life spreading slowly from this little planet throughout all space.

The End